KATY'S BOW

by Gini Graham Scott

Illustrations by

Nick Korolev

KATY'S BOW

One day, Katy started something really big. It began with a simple little bow.

Katy was heading home excited about the red bows she had made in school, when she saw Queenie, the Persian cat, who belonged to her next door neighbor, Mrs. Jones.

As Queenie held her tail high, Katy had an idea. She pulled one of her bows from her school bag and waved it, calling: "Here Queenie. Here Queenie."

Queenie bounded over, eager to swat the swinging bow. Katy bent down and snapped the bow around Queenie's neck.

"There! Now you look like a pretty Christmas package," Katy announced.

Queenie twisted around, trying to look at the strange object on her neck.

Skipper, the Yellow Lab puppy who lived down the block, saw Queenie wearing the bow. He gave a sharp "Yip!" of surprise and playfully chased after her, his tail wagging.

Scared by Skipper racing towards her, Queenie turned and sped off.

But Skipper ran faster. Just as he was about to catch up to her, Queenie saw a tall oak tree with spreading branches ahead. She scampered up, climbing from branch to branch.

Skipper sat on his haunches looking up at Queenie. He barked, his tail wagging, to show he wanted to play.

But he looked very big, so Queenie climbed higher and higher.

Skipper gazed longingly up the tree. Then, hungry, he headed home.

Queenie tried to back down the tree, but stopped. The ground below looked so far away, and she began yowling.

Katy walked over to the tree and looked up.

"Oh, you poor thing," she thought.

She ran across the street to Old Mr. Crockett house and knocked. Mr. Crockett opened the door, his spectacles perched on his head.

"There's a cat in the tree," Katy told him. "Can you get help?"

"Of course," Mr. Crockett said and called the fire department.

Soon, a fire truck arrived, followed by a police car. As the firefighters set up the ladder, Mrs. Jones, Queenie's owner, looked out her window to see what the commotion was all about.

Seeing Queenie in the tree, she ran out of her house and sped to the bottom of the tree next to Katy.

She looked up, moaning. "Oh, my poor Queenie."

Soon a crowd gathered to see why a fire truck and a police car were on the street.

Meanwhile, Skipper, back home, began jumping up and down at the window. He barked excitedly. When his owner, Mr. Anderson, heard him, he looked out the window, saw the huge crowd, and called the local TV station.

Soon TV reporters and camera crews arrived. They took pictures of the people, police officer, and firefighters, who were deciding how to get Queenie out of the tree.

As one firefighter went to get a ladder, Paul, the local newspaper reporter, headed to the scene with a photographer.

Just as their car turned the corner, Skipper, curious about the excitement, jumped through an open window. He ran across the lawn and into the street in front of Paul's car.

Quick as a flash, Paul stepped on the brake and swerved, as Skipper zipped across the street. But before Paul could stop, he hit the back of Mr. Anderson's van, and WHOOSH, it began rolling!

Faster and faster the van rolled, and at the intersection, BANG! it hit the back of the TV van, which began rolling, too, right into the light pole at the corner.

Uh, oh. CRUNCH. SNAP. SIZZLE. The wires and pole tumbled down.

SNAP
SIZZLE
CRUNCH
CAT 9 NEWS

Then, ZAP! All the neighborhood lights went off, and the street was in total darkness, except for the glow from the moon.

A few minutes later, two men in a local gas and electric company truck arrived to fix the wires. They climbed up a pole, while the firefighters set up their ladder to get Queenie down. At the same time, a dozen reporters and the camera crew went around interviewing everyone.

Just then, Katy's parents joined her at the tree.

"Why are you here in the dark?" her mother asked.

"And why is everyone in the street?" asked her father.

"Ummm, I think it all began when I put a bow around Queenie's neck and Skipper chased her," Katie replied.

Her parents looked bewildered. But before they could ask Katie anything more, a firefighter climbed down the ladder holding Queenie.

Mrs. Jones rushed over, gushing: "Oh, how can I thank you enough?"

She grabbed Queenie and hugged her tightly.

But where was the bow? It was no longer around Queenie's neck.

"How strange," Katy thought.

Then, she saw the bright red bow sitting on a pile of leaves at the bottom of the tree.

The bow almost seemed to be laughing at her, lit up by the light of the TV cameras that were filming Queenie's rescue.

"To think I started all this," Katy thought. "With just a single little bow."

She picked up the bow and started walking home, when Skipper came over, his tail wagging. He gazed at the bow and began pawing at her leg, as if to say: "Please give me the bow. Let's play some more."

Katy smiled and held up the bow, deciding what to do.

Then, she simply petted Skipper's head and walked over to one of the firefighters.

"Here's a bow for you," she said. "It's to say thank you for fixing everything after the bow started it all."

About the Author

GINI GRAHAM SCOTT, Ph.D., J.D., CEO of Changemakers Publishing and Writing, is an internationally known known writer, speaker, and workshop leader. She has published over 50 books with major publishers on various topics and has written over 3 dozen children's books. She is a member of the Society of Children's Book Writers and Illustrators. She does workshops on self-publishing and creativity, and she helps clients write books and self-publish them or find publishers and agents.

Her websites are
www.changemakerspublishingandwriting.com
and www.changemakerskids.com.

About the Illustrator

NICK KOROLEV was born and raised in New Jersey and started drawing recognizable animals at age four. By age 12 he was painting realistic seascapes and by 18 was doing pet portraits in pastels and oils professionally. Later he graduated with a BA in fine art. Specializing in wildlife, his work has won awards and been in many galleries, including the Smithsonian. Over the years, he extended his genres into illustration and cartooning. Presently he lives in Fisher, West Virginia with a tiger cat named Teddy and a black cat named Ninja. His "day jobs" include substitute teaching for two counties, and in the summer, he is the naturalist for the Lost River State Park.

He has a Facebook page at Nick Korolev Author/Artist,
is on LinkedIn, and has a website at www.korolevportfolio.com.

CHANGEMAKERS KIDS

3527 Mt. Diablo Blvd.
Lafayette, CA 94549
www.changemakerskids.com
changemakers@pacbell.net
(925) 385-0608

CPSIA information can be obtained
at www.ICGtesting.com
Printed in the USA
BVHW010918021020
590167BV00002B/3